Robert Heidbreder

illustrations by Marc Mongeau

TRADEWIND BOOKS

Vancouver • • London

To Dan and Dominique, two Shake-Awake friends—RH
To my children David, Matilde, Rosalie and Arthur
They're awake and my world is shaking!—MM

Shake-Awakes

WAKE-UP CALLS
for Grown-up use only

Precisely on the Dot

Precisely on the dot,
    right at 7:35,
the bed you're in will groan
    and burp itself alive.
It will gobble up what lies there—
                   GULP!

    the sheets, the pillows—it won't care.
Ten fingers, toes—
        GULP!

    all of you.
It's 7:34.
    What do you want to do?
    It isn't UP to me to say.
    It's really UP to you!

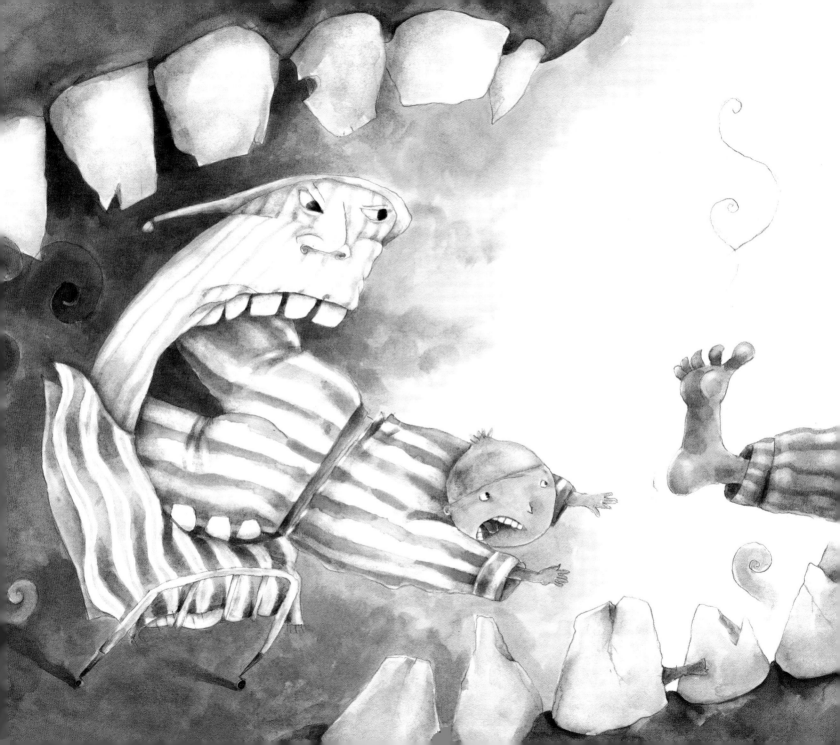

Lay Down Your Heads

Lay down your heads,
     sleepy ones,
     and tumble gently back to sleep.
Dream of monsters,
     witches,
        goblins,
           big sinkholes, stinky-deep.
See creepy-crawly creatures
           crinkling up your sheet.
For breakfast, lunch and dinner,
           dream you're eating wet concrete.
Or…
     toss aside the covers
        from your ghoulish beds.
        Let butterflies and sunbeams
        stream into your heads.

The Sleep Bugs

Rise and shine.
     Shine and rise.
Shake the sleep bugs
     from your eyes.
If you sleep another wink,
     the eyeball bugs will surely think
     you're their breakfast food today.

     What will happen?
       (We can't say.)

So shine and rise.
     Rise and shine.
Before those bugs begin to...
          DINE!

The Toy Trolls

SHHH! SHHH! Don't wake up now.
 Toy trolls are in your room.
  They're ghastly green
   and ghostly grim, as if they're from a tomb.
 Their feet stink strongly of manure.
  (They've never had a pedicure.)
 They hate clean water, suds and soap.
  (They smell of rotting cantaloupe.)
 They grab your toys, rub them with stench,
  then smash them with a greasy wrench.
 So don't wake now.
  They might see you.
But you can scare them. Look—SHAMPOO!
  Jump UP fast. Don't be slow!
  Scrub those trolls!
  GO! GO! GO!

Boreas the Wind

Here's Boreas the Wind,
    OₒₒO ᴏᴏᴏₒₒO ᴏᴏₒₒₒᴏᴏᴏᴏO
blowing from the North
    to shiver, quiver you,
to whirl your covers,
    freeze your hair,
    to strip you naked, cold-bum bare.
Beware its breath like icy snow.
    No one escapes its wintry blow.
No one escapes its raging wrath
    unless you flee out of its path.
Before you feel its glacial slam—
jump **UP**,
    get dressed…and…
    SCRAM! SCRAM! SCRAM!

Knock Knock Knock

Rattle Rattle Rattle
   Knock Knock Knock
   We think you must have locked the lock.
   Or is the door jammed stuck today?
   Maybe we should go away.
Jiggle Jiggle Jiggle
   Nudge Nudge Nudge
   Your door sure doesn't want to budge.
   We've got this package addressed to you.
   But we can't deliver it.
   We can't get through.
   You won't get **UP**.
   Hey, it's okay.
   We'll let the postman cart it away.
   There he goes, before our eyes.
   Wave good-bye to your surprise!

The Cabbage Scourge

In your closet, about to emerge,
is **ME**—the rotten **CABBAGE SCOURGE**.
My head's red cabbage.
My feet, blood beets.
My bum and belly, rutabaga treats.
My nose, a radish.
My eyes, black peas.
HOORAY! I think I'm gonna sneeze!
Out will spray my veggie goo.
Then you'll smell like mouldy stew.
So don't get **UP**. Don't touch that door.
I might drip down onto the floor.
Between the boards, I'll disappear
where I can't spread my smelly fear.
No, don't get **UP**.
I'll count to three.
'Cause in three counts...I will be **FREE**!

We've tried our best.

Now here's the last.

They'll shake-awake…

…at our

BUGLE
BLAST!

Bugle Blast

(to the rhythm of "Reveille")

Time to get **U**P.
　Time to get **U**P.
　　Time to get **UP** this morning.
Better get **U**P.
　Better get **U**P.
　　Better get **UP** we're warning.
We'll give you five.
　We'll give you five.
　　　1 − 2 − 3 − 4 − 5 is past.
Okay, here comes...
　the dreaded...
　　bugle... **BLAST!**

BRUUUUUL

They're **not** Up *yet!*

Still sound asleep.

Big slug-a-bugs in a heap.

Time to do...

...whatever it takes.

Let's get that book...

WAKE-Up CALLS
for children's use only

Gosh! Oh Gosh!

Our dream! Our dream!
    It's really true.
    A **TRAMPOLINE**—brand-new from you!
Now we can spring high, bounce about,
    shriek with laughter, scream and shout.
               WHEEEEEEEEEEEEEEEE!
GOSH!
    We woke you?
GOSH!
    It's your **BED**?
GOSH!
    The dream stayed in our head.
GOSH!
    That dream was hunky-dory!
    Sorry to wake you.
           Sorry.
               SORRY!

Accidentally!

OH NO! OH NO!
      We think it broke.
      It sizzle-fizzled, billowing smoke.
      Milk *accidentally* spilled on the keys,
      and we *accidentally* dropped grilled cheese.
      Accidentally we cracked the screen
      while trying to shine it with Vaseline.
      And as we polished, pulled and tugged,
      it *accidentally* came unplugged.
      It whirred and twirred and stirred a bit
      before it—**BOOOOM-BANG**—up and quit.

We hate to wake you **UP**, wide-eyed,
      but we think...
            the computer...
                  kinda...
                       died?

The Stuffie News

HEADLINE NEWS: OUR STUFFIES CAN FLY!

Baby beluga soars through the sky!

Kangaroo takes to the air!

And monster mouse rides grizzly bear!

We fell asleep. They were quiet.

When we got up: an air-borne riot.

Look!

>They're in your room,

>zooming around,

>seeking a runway to touch down.

OH WOW!

>They're heading straight your way.

>Rise and shine! Don't dare delay.

Get **UP**! Get **UP**!

No longer snooze.

Get **UP** and share **THE STUFFIE NEWS!**

Scuttle Scuttle Scuttle

scuttle scuttle scuttle
   claw claw claw
      rustle rustle rustle
         paw paw paw
            scratch scratch scratch
               gnaw gnaw gnaw

A RAT! A RAT!

   We saw a rat,
   bloated, buck-toothed, wobbly-fat.
Wake **UP**! Wake **UP**! Stop playing dead!
   We think a rat's beneath your bed!
   Get **UP** and grab it. Trap it now…
   before it bites us.

            OW! OW! OW!

Surprise! Surprise!

Surprise! Surprise!
     Here's breakfast for you!
     Open **UP**. Let us come through.
          These trays are tricky, hard to hold.
          Your scrumptious toast is getting cold.
Open! Open!
     We're losing our grip.
     Everything is starting to slip.
        CRASH! SMASH!
        SPLISHITY-SPLASH!
OOOOOOOOPS! Too late!
Your food's on the floor.
DON'T open **UP** now....
You should have before.

Slimy, Slinky Goo

Hey! Hey! Wake UP!
    We lost the remote.
        It toppled in the toilet and it sure can't float.
    We tried to fish it from the bowl,
        but it got stuck tight down the hole.
    So then we flushed and flushed and flushed,
        but swampy water gushed and gushed.
    It's flooded the bathroom.
        It's oozing toward you.
Get UP and STOp IT whatever you do!
Get UP and STOP the slimy goo!
'Cause the slimy, slinky goo
smells just like—*whew*—pee-yew!

Morning Elves

Hello! Hello!
    We're morning elves,
        with sunny eyes,
    to help you greet the bright sunrise.

An easy day, a breezy day
    we wish you as we softly spray
    our morning mist above your head
    to nudge you gently from your bed.

We pause only a teeny while.
    Wake and show your new-day smile.

'Cause…
    if you don't, we might turn mean,
    more mean than anything you've seen.
    We won't reveal what we will do…

    but think of CLOUDBURSTS over you.
    Imagine blankets dripping wet,
    as deeply drenched as they can get.
    Imagine cold germs gripping you.
    Imagine this: ACHOO! ACHOO!
    So our advice is: DO NOT WAIT.
    Get UP before it is TOO LATE!
                NOW!

Nothing worked!
That's it!
OKAY!
They'll wish they woke up right away.

Off to the kitchen…

for pots, pans, spoons.

It's time to play…

…our **SHAKE-AWAKE** tunes.

Ladies and gentlemen, give a hand…

…to the one and only

TIN PAN BAND!

The Tin Pan Band

Spoons strike pots:
> BANG BANG BANG

Feet march in place:
> CLOMP CLOMP CLOMP

Lids crash together:
> CLANG CLANG CLANG

Ready…set…
> STOMP STOMP STOMP
> BANG BANG BANG
> CLOMP CLOMP CLOMP
> CLANG CLANG CLANG
> STOMP STOMP STOMP
> BANG BANG BANG
> CLOMP CLOMP CLOMP
> CLANG CLANG CLANG
> STOMP STOMP STOMP

The Tin Pan Band has marched to your room
to get you **UP** with a Tin Pan **BOOM**!
To get you tuned to a Tin Pan day!
And till you're **UP**, WE WON'T GO AWAY!
And repeat:
The Tin Pan Band has marched to your room
to get you **UP** with a Tin Pan **BOOM**!
To get you tuned to a Tin Pan day!
And till you're **UP**, WE WON'T GO AWAY!

Finally, they're up...and YIKES!
Oh dear.
RUN...don't march.
GET OUTTA HERE!